Boo and Ted's Amazing Adventures

Beach Rescue

Written by John Dunn

Illustrated by Holly Withers

For my two daughters. They always insisted on a bed time story and I made this one up for them several years ago. -JD

ISBN 978-1-7364223-1-1 (hardcover)
ISBN 978-1-7364223-0-4 (paperback)
ISBN 978-1-7364223-2-8 (Ebook)

For permission requests or ordering information, contact:

John Dunn
2358 University Avenue Box 434
San Diego, CA 92104
johndunn20@gmail.com

Special thanks to Denise Vega and Holly Withers, who made this book possible. Denise taught me all about the art of writing picture books and helped me shape this story. Holly's fun and colorful illustrations make the book come alive. I love her illustrations!

"I'm bored," sighed Boo. Mama and the girls had just left the house. They wouldn't be back until 3pm.

"Already?" said Ted. "Well, I'm tired." Ted found some shade and closed his eyes.

Ted had just started dreaming, when Boo began shaking him.

"Wake up Ted! The weather's perfect. Let's go to the beach!"

"No way!" said Ted. "That's a terrible idea. It's way too dangerous. We could get run over by a car. We could get a thorn stuck in our paw." Ted paused. "We could get in big trouble with Mama!!"

BEEP! BEEP!

"Too late, our ride's here! I found Mama's phone and ordered an Uber." Boo jumped up and down with excitement. She unlocked the gate and ran out the door.

"Come on. It'll be an adventure!"

"Wait!! Don't leave me here by myself!" Ted shouted, running after Boo.

They jumped into the car.

Their driver was too busy singing along with the radio to notice his unusual passengers.

Once they got to the beach, Boo raced
around playing and splashing in the water.

Ted sat on the sand biting his nails nervously.

Finally, Boo took a break.
She flopped down next to Ted.

"This is fun! Come join me."

"No thanks. A wave might knock us into the ocean.
We could get sand in our eyes." Ted paused.
"We could step on a sharp seashell!"

Suddenly, they heard a cry out in the water.

"Help! Help!"

"Oh no!" shouted Ted. "That kid is in trouble. Where's the lifeguard?"

They looked around. But there were no lifeguards!

And no one else seemed to hear the cry for help!

"What do we do?" Ted looked at Boo. "That kid is too far out for us to swim!"

"There's no time to lose. We'll have to save him ourselves!!" Boo exclaimed.

Boo saw a jet ski on the beach near the water.

"Follow me!" Boo shouted.

"It's pretty far out there. Shouldn't we wait to see if someone else can help?"

But Boo had already raced over to the jet ski and started pushing it toward the water.

Ted ran after Boo. Together they pushed the jet ski into the water.

VROOM! VROOM!

The jet ski crashed through the waves. Ted reached out his paw and grabbed the boy.

A crowd gathered on the beach watching the rescue.

"Did you see that?!" exclaimed a woman.

"Amazing!" shouted a man.

"Thank you," said the boy's mother breathlessly.
"How can I ever repay you?"

"Arf, Arf," Boo barked politely.

The mother laughed. "Of course, a dog treat!"
She handed a treat to Boo and Ted from her purse.

Ted glanced at the mother's watch and gasped.
"Oh no! It's almost three o'clock!! Let's go Boo!"

Boo and Ted took off running.

"We'll never make it home in time," said Ted, panting after running only one block.

Boo saw an electric scooter parked on the sidewalk. "Hop on Ted!" They jumped on the scooter and raced toward home.

Boo revved the scooter to max speed and raced down the street.

They left the scooter on the sidewalk and ran into the yard.

"Phew, I'm exhausted, but we beat them home,"
Ted drank some water, then collapsed in the yard.
"We saved that boy. I was scared, but I'm sure glad
we decided to help."

"I'm proud of you Ted. You were brave even though
you were scared. We sure make a great team!"

Just then Mama and the girls pulled up.

"Look at those lazy dogs!" Cecilia exclaimed as she walked through the gate.

"Right where we left them," added Luci.

"I could have sworn I locked the gate this morning," Mama mumbled shaking her head as she put down her purse. "Hey, how did my phone get outside?"

"I feel bad." said Mama. "These dogs have been cooped up here all day. I better take them for a long walk."

Boo jumped up excitedly and got ready to go.

Ted did not.

The End

Made in the USA
Las Vegas, NV
13 January 2022